Claudia
the Accessories
Fairy

Special thanks to Sue Mongredien

ISBN 978-0-545-48485-5

12 11 10 9 8 7 6 5 4 3 2 1   13 14 15 16 17 18/0

Printed in China   68

This edition first printing, July 2013

Claudia
the Accessories
Fairy

by Daisy Meadows

SCHOLASTIC INC.

I'm the king of designer fashion,
Looking stylish is my passion.
Ice Blue's the name of my fashion line,
The designs are fabulous and they're all mine!

Some people think my clothes are odd,
But I will get the fashion world's nod.
Fashion Fairy magic will make my dream come true —
Soon everyone will wear Ice Blue!

Contents

A Hole Lot of Trouble

"Here we are," Mr. Walker said, parking the car at Tippington Fountains Shopping Center. He glanced over to where his daughter, Rachel, and her best friend, Kirsty Tate, were sitting in the backseat. "I know you girls were here yesterday, but I need to pick up a shirt. I'll be as quick as I can."

"Don't worry, Dad," Rachel said, exchanging a secret smile with Kirsty as they got out of the car. "We don't mind at all. Take as long as you need!"

It was the second day of school vacation, and Kirsty was staying with Rachel's family. Whenever the two friends got together, magical things always seemed to happen — and they certainly had yesterday! Rachel's mom

had taken the girls to the new mall to be part of the opening-day celebration. There were lots of free activities and a whole parade with colorful floats. It had been really fun and exciting . . . especially when the girls found themselves whisked off to Fairyland and thrown into an exciting, brand-new fairy adventure. Hooray!

"I hope we meet another fairy today," Kirsty whispered eagerly to Rachel, as they made their way through the parking lot to the elevators.

"Oh, me too," Rachel replied. "Yesterday was amazing. But you know what Queen Titania always says: We can't go looking for magic. We have to wait for it to come to us." She grinned. "I just hope it finds us again soon!"

The three of them went up in the elevator. "First floor," a voice from the speaker announced after a few moments. "Welcome to Tippington Fountains Shopping Center!" The doors opened to reveal the shopping mall before them. The store doors sparkled with shiny chrome handles, glass elevators rose smoothly

between floors, and a large central
fountain sprayed in the middle of a wide
blue pool, with smaller fountains bubbling
all around it. Rachel smiled as she and
Kirsty gazed at the fountain display.

That was the spot where they'd seen
Phoebe the Fashion Fairy yesterday —
and where their new fairy adventure
had begun.

Of course, they'd met Phoebe before —
they'd had a very exciting adventure
with her when they'd helped all the
Party Fairies on a secret mission. But
Kirsty and Rachel hadn't realized that
Phoebe had a whole team of Fashion
Fairies who assisted her throughout the
fairy kingdom and in the human world.

Yesterday, Phoebe had invited the girls
to Fairyland to see the special fairy
fashion show they were putting on. And
that was when everything had gone
wrong. . . .

Kirsty shuddered as she remembered
how Jack Frost and his goblins had
appeared at the show uninvited. They
then proceeded to mess up the whole
thing! Jack Frost had strutted in wearing
an outfit from his own clothing label, Ice

Blue, and he used a bolt of icy magic to steal seven magical objects that belonged to the Fashion Fairies. Kirsty and Rachel immediately returned to the human world and helped Miranda the Beauty Fairy rescue her magic lipstick, a very special lipstick that made sure everyone had a beautiful, natural smile. But there were still six magical objects left to find.

"What do you think of this hat, girls?" Mr. Walker asked, pulling Kirsty from her thoughts. She and Rachel turned to see that he'd stopped at Winter Woolies and was holding up a black ski hat.

"It looks like what I need to keep my head warm now that the weather's colder."

"I like it," Rachel said. "Why don't you try it on?"

Mr. Walker pulled the hat onto his head. To their surprise, his head went

right through the top of it. "Oh!" he cried, startled. "This wasn't made very well." He took the hat off to reveal a giant hole in the wool knitting.

"How strange," he said. "I didn't notice that before."

The lady working in the booth looked surprised, too. "I'm so sorry," she said. "There must have been a loose thread in that one. Please try another."

But when Mr. Walker tried a second hat on — a navy blue one, this time — the same thing happened again. And he wasn't the only person who was having trouble. A nearby woman had just bought a thick red scarf. But when she wrapped it around her neck, the wool unravelled and left long strands dangling at each end!

"I don't understand,"

the lady in the booth said. She turned
pink and looked flustered. "I'm so sorry.
There must be a bad batch. Let me find
you another scarf."

Rachel and Kirsty exchanged a look.
Could this have something to do with
the Fashion Fairies' missing magical
objects?

Then Kirsty glanced down at her watch and gasped. "Look, Rachel," she whispered, pointing. "The hands on my watch are moving backward. Something *very* weird is going on!"

Magic Sparkles

The girls stared at Kirsty's watch as the second hand ticked the wrong way around the face. That *was* weird. "It definitely feels like there's magic in the air," Rachel whispered. "Magic that isn't working very well. We need to investigate!"

Rachel went over to her dad, who was trying on a third hat. "Dad, can Kirsty

and I go off on our own for a little while?" she asked.

"Of course," Mr. Walker said, just as the hat ripped apart at the seam. "I'm not having much luck with hats today, that's for sure," he grumbled, taking it off again. He glanced up at a large clock on the wall of the shopping center. "Let's meet back here in an hour."

The girls agreed and waved good-bye, keeping an eye out for other strange events as they walked away.

"We could start looking for things to use in our outfits for the design

competition while we're here," Kirsty
suggested.

"Good idea," Rachel
said. "Then we can
work on them this
afternoon, so we'll be
ready for tomorrow."

At the grand opening
of the mall the day
before, Jessica Jarvis, a famous model,
had announced a special competition.
Kids could design and make their own
outfits! They needed to show the clothes
they'd created to the judges tomorrow
afternoon. Then the winning designers
would get to wear the outfits in a charity
fashion show at the end of the week.

"I think I'll make something rainbow-
colored and sparkly," Rachel said

thoughtfully. "It'll remind me of our very first magical adventure with the Rainbow Fairies — and all the wonderful fairy friends we've made since then."

"That sounds great," Kirsty said. "I might make a dress out of flowy scarves sewn together. Something bright and patterned would be nice."

"Let's look in here," Rachel suggested, pointing to a nearby shop named Finishing Touch.

The friends walked toward the shop just

as two teenage girls came out. One had
a pretty new bag on her shoulder and the
other was fastening a new necklace
around her neck. But just then, the strap
on the first girl's bag broke, sending it
tumbling to the ground. And seconds
later, the other
girl's necklace
snapped. Shiny
purple beads
cascaded
down and
scattered
everywhere!
  "Oh, no!"
the girls both
cried. "How did
that happen?"

Kirsty and Rachel
ran to help pick
up the fallen
beads, but
it was no
use. The
necklace was
beyond repair.

"Come on, let's get a refund," one of
the teenagers said as they went back
into the shop. "Brand-new accessories
shouldn't just fall apart like that!"

Rachel and Kirsty followed them
inside, and Kirsty headed for a rack
of scarves. To her disappointment, the
only scarves in stock seemed to be blue.
There was nothing at all like the bright
patterns she'd hoped to find.

Rachel was also finding the store to be
a letdown. The jewelry seemed to have
lost its sparkle, and some pieces had
missing stones or broken clasps. None of
it was right for the outfit she had in mind
for the competition.

"This is really weird," she heard the
shop assistant saying in confusion. "All
our accessories looked beautiful when I

put them out this morning. But somehow they've become dull or broken since then." Rachel headed toward a display of necklaces. Surely there would be *some* sparkly jewelry there, right? She sped up as she spotted something glinting from between the beads. Then, as she reached for the necklaces, she almost jumped out of her skin. The sparkly jewel she thought she'd

seen wasn't a jewel at all. In fact, it had just flown right off the necklace and into the air!

Rachel gasped in delight as she realized what she was seeing. A fairy!

"Hello!" said the fairy, smiling at Rachel.
She was wearing a sparkly purple skirt, a
pink top, and a blue cardigan. Elegant
bangles and a headband with a big
flower topped off the outfit. Rachel
recognized her as Claudia the Accessories
Fairy, one of the seven Fashion Fairies
she and Kirsty had met the day before.

"Hello," Rachel replied, smiling back. She glanced around to find Kirsty, who was still looking through the rack of blue scarves.

"Kirsty!" she whispered. "Over here!"

Kirsty's eyes lit up when she saw Claudia hovering in midair, a bright spark of light in the gloomy shop. She hurried over immediately.

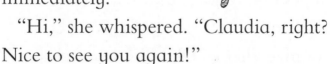

"Hi," she whispered. "Claudia, right? Nice to see you again!"

"Nice to see you, too," Claudia said, her wings glittering as they fluttered.

24

"I really need your help, girls. Since
Jack Frost took my necklace, its magic has
switched to reverse. Instead of making
sure that fashion accessories look perfectly
pretty, the magic is working the other
way. Now accessories look horrible!
Even worse, they keep breaking and
falling apart!"

"So that's
why all
those hats
were torn,"
Rachel
figured
out. "And
why the
teenagers' bag
and necklace broke
earlier, too."

"And that must be why my watch seems to be telling time backward," Kirsty realized. "What a mess! We'll definitely help you look for your necklace, Claudia."

"Thank you." The little fairy beamed

 and flew up to balance on a rack of necklaces. "Well, I've looked all over this store and it isn't here. And unfortunately,

until it's back with me where it belongs, everyone's accessories will break or just look awful. We have to keep looking!"

Just then, the three of them heard a loud voice coming from outside the shop.

"Come to the Ice Blue booth for the last word in fashion!" the voice boasted.

Kirsty, Rachel, and Claudia stiffened at the words. Ice Blue? That was the label Jack Frost had given to his clothing line. It couldn't be a coincidence, could it?

They rushed out of the store to see what was going on.

There was Jack Frost himself, shouting
into a megaphone and dressed from head
to toe in a silvery-blue outfit. His jacket
had spikes on the shoulders and elbows,
and there was a frosty pattern on his
pants. He was standing in front of a
booth decorated with blue banners and
piled high with lots of different blue
accessories.

"Wow — he's a fast worker," Kirsty commented. "That booth wasn't even there when we came into the store a few minutes ago."

"He must have used magic to help set it up," Claudia whispered from where she was hiding in Rachel's pocket. "So maybe he has my magic necklace — let's go and see!"

The girls left the store with Claudia peeking out of Rachel's pocket. There was already a crowd around Jack Frost's booth, rummaging through the hats, scarves, key rings, bags, purses, and jewelry on sale there. All of the products had the same logo — a bright blue silhouette of Jack Frost, showing off his big pointy nose and spiky beard.

"No need to push, there's plenty for everyone!" called one of the booth assistants. Kirsty nudged Rachel as she noticed that the assistants had green skin and long noses. They were goblins! All of them wore matching T-shirts with the same Ice Blue logo. They kept very busy, dealing with lots of customers at once.

Being careful not to be noticed by Jack Frost or the goblins, the girls squeezed through the crowd and pretended they

were customers, too. They searched
through the boxes of necklaces hoping
to spot a magical shimmer, which
would mean they had found Claudia's
necklace.

"You have very nice blue jeans," one
of the goblins said,
casting a sly look
at Rachel from
under his Ice
Blue baseball
cap. "Ice Blue is
the place to come if
you're looking for the
very best blue accessories, you know."

"It's too bad about your nasty red skirt
and shirt, though, miss," a second goblin
said rudely to Kirsty. "We don't have
anything to go with red. Yuck!"

Kirsty was annoyed by the goblin's insult, but she knew she shouldn't draw attention to herself by arguing. Biting her tongue, she turned away and looked at a different part of the booth.

"Girls, let's go," Claudia whispered from Rachel's pocket. "I don't think the necklace is here, after all."

Rachel and Kirsty struggled to get out of the crowd, which was now even bigger than before. Once they were a safe distance away, Rachel asked, "Why don't you think the necklace was in the Ice Blue booth, Claudia? Jack Frost and his goblins were definitely working there."

"I know, but didn't you hear what the goblin said?" Claudia asked. "They didn't have anything to match Kirsty's top. My necklace should make sure that there are *always* matching accessories nearby, even if the rest of its magic isn't working properly." She gave a little sigh of frustration. "That means the necklace must be somewhere else. . . . But where?"

Follow That Goblin!

As the girls discussed where to look next, Rachel noticed a new goblin arrive at the booth. He was carrying boxes of Ice Blue merchandise.

"Coming through, coming through," he shouted, shoving past the customers. "More amazing accessories coming through!"

One of the goblins in the booth looked relieved to see the newcomer. "About time," he snapped. "What took you so long? We already sold out of baseball hats. Here, take this empty box away with you."

"I wonder where they're getting all those accessories from," Rachel said to the others. "They must be using magic to make them so quickly. What do you think, Claudia?"

Claudia brightened. "You're right," she said. "They're using magic from my necklace, I bet!"

"Let's follow the goblin and see where he goes," Kirsty suggested. "If we can find out where the Ice Blue accessories are coming from, we might find your necklace, too."

"Good thinking," Claudia agreed. "But we can't let the goblins see us or they'll get suspicious. I'll turn you both into fairies. Then it will be easier for us all to stay out of sight. Let's find a quiet spot, so I can work some magic."

The girls didn't need to be told twice. They both loved being fairies — nothing beat fluttering your wings and taking off into the air!

Kirsty and Rachel quickly huddled
behind a large Ice Blue display. Claudia
waved her wand and sent a stream of
purple sparkles into the air. The magic
sparkles swirled
around the girls
and, in the
blink of an
eye, they felt
themselves
shrinking
smaller and
smaller, until
they were the same
size as Claudia. They
were fairies again! The girls joyfully
fluttered their shimmering wings and
soared into the air, chasing the goblin
with the empty cardboard box.

The goblin exited the mall and turned into a deserted alley. The three friends quietly followed him through the back door of a building. They hid in a high, dark corner as he pressed a button on the wall to call the elevator. Then they slipped into the elevator behind him, being careful not to be seen.

The goblin pressed a button marked "B," and the elevator plunged downward.

"Basement," a robotic voice announced once the elevator had stopped moving. The doors jerked apart, and the goblin walked out.

Kirsty, Rachel, and Claudia flew after him and found themselves in a large workshop full of goblins busily working at noisy machines. The fairies flitted up to a corner filled with cobwebs. There, they perched on a ceiling beam to get a better view of the room.

"Wow — they set up a whole factory to make the Ice Blue accessories," Kirsty said under her breath. She stared at the rows of goblins using sewing machines, plastic molds, scissors, and glue guns. Elsewhere, there were giant rolls of blue fabric and boxes of finished products stacked in tall towers.

"Jack Frost must have used his ice magic to make all this equipment," Claudia said, looking dazed. "He really *is* serious about his fashion company, isn't he? He obviously wants everyone to look just like him."

Rachel let out a little cry of excitement as she noticed something. "Look!" she whispered. "The goblin in charge — he's wearing your magic necklace, Claudia!"

True Blue, Through and Through!

There was no disguising the magic
necklace. It shimmered with all the colors
of the rainbow from around the neck of
the tallest goblin, who was bossing
everyone else around. "Keep moving on
those hats, guys," he yelled down one aisle
of the workshop. "How are we doing on
gloves? Let me check the quality."

Kirsty, Rachel, and Claudia watched him stride down to the glove-making table. He angrily picked up a pair of gloves. "*Green* gloves? Weren't you listening to Jack Frost? Everything's got to be blue, you fools. You'll have to throw these away and start again."

The goblins at the glove-making table looked disgruntled. "But we like green," one of them said with a sulky pout. "It's much better than blue."

"No arguing!" snapped the tall goblin. "While I'm wearing this magic necklace, *I'm* in charge, so you'll do as I say. Now get back to making blue gloves right now — or I'll tell Jack Frost how lazy you are!"

Listening to their conversation gave Kirsty an idea. "Claudia, could you use your fairy magic to disguise Rachel and me as goblin workers?" she asked. "I'm wondering if, between us, we can make the supervisor decide he doesn't want to be in charge anymore."

Rachel's eyes lit up. "Oh, yes!" She giggled. "And once he takes off that necklace . . ."

"I'll pounce!" Claudia finished with a grin. "Let's give it a try. If we go back to the elevator area, I can turn you both into goblins!"

They quietly flew out of the workshop and back into the elevator, where nobody could see them. Then Claudia waved her wand, and there was a bright flash of magic and a cloud of purple smoke. When

the smoke cleared, Kirsty and Rachel laughed as they saw that they now looked just like the other goblins on the factory floor. "Time to get to work," Kirsty said with a grin.

"Actually, time to stir up some trouble!" Rachel replied with a wink.

The two of them split up and joined the other goblins, who were working busily. Kirsty went to the assembly line, where a team of goblins was producing scarves, while Rachel went to the jewelry-making table nearby.

"I'm not a big fan of all this blue, you know," Kirsty muttered to the goblins closest to her. "I'd much rather wear a *green* scarf, wouldn't you?

Goblin green — everyone knows that's the best color, right?"

"Goblin green is definitely *my* favorite color," agreed a grumpy-looking goblin with pointy ears.

"It's a shame we can only make blue things when there are so many other colors in the rainbow," Rachel added innocently. "You'd look really handsome in purple, for example," she said, pointing at the goblin closest to her. "And as for you — well, a yellow scarf or hat would really bring out the color of your eyes." She said this to a

small, shy-looking goblin, and he
blushed with pride.

"Do you think so?"
he said happily. "I
do like yellow,
I have to say."

"Red's my
favorite color,"
another goblin
added. "It
makes me think
of strawberry jam.
And who ever heard of
blue strawberry jam?"

Soon, all the goblins were joining in:
"Green's definitely best."

"I'd like brown, to match my teeth."

"Orange clothes look lovely on green
skin, I think."

The supervisor was starting to look annoyed. He blew a whistle to make everyone stop talking. "That's enough!" he roared. "You're supposed to be working, not chatting. Silence!"

Kirsty dropped her scissors with a clatter. "I'm not doing any more work unless we can use different colors," she said daringly.

"Me neither," Rachel agreed, folding her arms. "I'm going on strike."

As she said the words, she felt her heart thump. If all the other goblins went back to work, then their plan would fail. She

and Kirsty might even be thrown out of
the workshop — and then they wouldn't
have any chance of getting the necklace.

Thankfully, it seemed the goblins had
all had enough of being bossed around,
too. All across the workshop, there was
the clatter of tools being put down. Every
single goblin put his nose in the air.

"I'm not working either," said one.

"We want colors!" said another.

"We want colors, we want colors!" chorused another group of goblins, stomping their feet in rhythm.

In a matter of seconds, the entire goblin workforce was chanting along and stomping feet. "We want colors, we want colors!"

One of the goblins opened a large cupboard and took out rolls of bright fabric. "Spots! Stripes! Flowers!" he cried happily.

"Red! Yellow! Green! Purple!" other goblins yelled, grabbing the fabrics they wanted to use.

The supervisor looked close to tears. Kirsty felt a little sorry for him, but she knew they had to stick to their plan if they were going to get Claudia's necklace back.

"Oh, no. Jack Frost's not going to be happy if he comes in and sees what's happening here," she said loudly.

"And to think he trusted you with the magic necklace," Rachel said to the supervisor, shaking her head.

"He's going to be especially angry with you!"

"I can't take it anymore!" the supervisor yelled, ripping the necklace from his neck. "I quit!"

Finishing Touches

Several goblins grabbed at the magic necklace as soon as the supervisor took it off, but Claudia was too quick for them all. Much to the goblins' surprise, she darted in, grabbed the necklace, and flew out of reach. "The game's over, boys," she said sweetly as the necklace shrank down to its fairy size. Then she waved

her wand, and the Ice Blue accessories
changed to all the colors of the rainbow.

The goblins cheered . . . but then their
faces fell as they realized what this
meant for them.

"Jack Frost is going to be so mad at
us." One gulped. "Quick! Let's get back
to Fairyland before he sees what we've
done." And in the next moment, all the
goblins had hurried out of the room. Just
two goblins remained, and they were
quickly changing back into girls.

Kirsty and Rachel grinned as Claudia turned three happy loops in the air to celebrate.

"Thank you so much, girls!" she said as she floated down toward them. "Your plan was genius. Now let's head back to the accessories shop where we met. With the help of my magic necklace, I'll make sure that everything in there looks gorgeous again."

As soon as Rachel and Kirsty were

back in the mall, they realized that
Claudia's magic was already working.
The crowd had vanished from around
the Ice Blue booth and they saw Jack
Frost desperately bellowing into his
megaphone, trying to attract customers.
When it was clear that nobody was
coming to buy anything, he
threw the megaphone
to the ground and
stomped off
furiously. "I'll
make everyone
wear Ice Blue
somehow," he
fumed.

"Not today, you
won't," Claudia said
with a smile, once he was out of earshot.

She tucked herself in Kirsty's pocket as they went into the Finishing Touch store again. Kirsty noticed with excitement that swirls of sparkly fairy magic were coming from Claudia's necklace and spreading around all the accessories.

In the blink of an eye, the shop was transformed. The dull, broken accessories were gone, and in their place were colorful scarves, hats, bags, and jewelry.

"That's *much* better!" Claudia smiled. "I'd better fly now, girls. Thanks again. And good luck with the fashion competition tomorrow. You know the Fashion Fairies will be rooting for you!"

"Bye, Claudia,"
Rachel said.
"Hope we see you
again soon."

"Good-bye,"
Kirsty added.
"And thank you. I
know making my
costume is going to
be much easier now
that there are so many
pretty scarves to choose from!"

Claudia vanished in a swirl of glittering
fairy dust, and Kirsty remembered to
check her watch. "It's working again!"
she said in relief. "Oh, but we only have
fifteen minutes before we meet your dad,
Rachel. We'd better choose something
for our outfits and head back."

"I know just what I'm going to do for mine," Rachel said, picking up a pack of glittery fabric paints. "After today, I'm tired of wearing blue. I'm going to make these jeans extra special by adding rainbow-colored patterns on them."

"Great idea," Kirsty said, sorting through the rack of scarves. She held up some striped scarves in bright colors.

"And these are perfect for my dress. Hooray!"

Once they'd paid for the scarves and paints, the two happy friends set off to meet Mr. Walker. They had the design competition tomorrow *and* the fashion show at the end of the week to look forward to.

"Oh, and look," Rachel said, pointing

to a sign that had just been put up in the mall. "There's a design competition workshop here tomorrow morning. That sounds like fun, too. What a busy week we're having!"

"Fun, fairies, and fashion — it sounds perfect to me." Kirsty laughed. "I can't wait to see what happens next!"

RAINBOW
magic™
THE FASHION FAIRIES

The girls helped Claudia find her
magic necklace.
Now it's time for Kirsty and Rachel to help

Tyra
the Designer Fairy!

Read on for a special sneak peek. . . .

Funny Fashions

"I can't wait for the design competition workshop to start," said Kirsty Tate, peeking into her bag with excitement. "I have my colorful scarves, and I'm going to sew them into a floaty dress."

"It will be great!" said her best friend, Rachel Walker. "I'm going to paint a glittery rainbow on my old jeans."

"And I'm going to have lunch with my friend Moira," said Mrs. Walker. "So we are all in store for an enjoyable day!"

They were standing inside the new Tippington Fountains Shopping Center. Kirsty was staying with Rachel for the school break, and they had been having a very exciting time ever since the new mall had opened. A design competition had been announced on the opening day, and the girls had been working on their ideas ever since. After the workshop, all the creations would be judged, and the winners would model their clothes in a fashion show at the end of the week.

"Let's go this way," said Mrs. Walker. "I told Moira I'd meet her outside the wedding-dress shop, Top Hats & Tiaras."

They walked along slowly, looking from

one side to the other at all the exciting stores. Then Rachel nudged Kirsty.

"Look at that lady over there," she said. "She's wearing one pant leg long and the other one is short."

"And her son only has one sock on," said Kirsty. "That's strange."

"New fashions always seem strange at first," said Mrs. Walker with a laugh. "Look, there's Moira over there, and she has safety pins on her cardigan instead of buttons. What will the fashion designers think of next?"

As Mrs. Walker went to give Moira a hug, Kirsty and Rachel exchanged a glance.

"These aren't funny new fashions," said Rachel. "It's Jack Frost and his goblins causing trouble!"

RAINBOW magic

These activities are magical!
Play dress-up, send friendship notes, and much more!

SCHOLASTIC
www.scholastic.com
www.rainbowmagiconline.com

HiT entertainment

RMACTIV3

RAINBOW magic™

SPECIAL EDITION

Three Books in Each One—
More Rainbow Magic Fun!

Joy the Summer Vacation Fairy
Holly the Christmas Fairy
Kylie the Carnival Fairy
Stella the Star Fairy
Shannon the Ocean Fairy
Trixie the Halloween Fairy
Gabriella the Snow Kingdom Fairy
Juliet the Valentine Fairy
Mia the Bridesmaid Fairy
Flora the Dress-Up Fairy
Paige the Christmas Play Fairy
Emma the Easter Fairy
Cara the Camp Fairy
Destiny the Rock Star Fairy
Belle the Birthday Fairy
Olympia the Games Fairy
Selena the Sleepover Fairy
Cheryl the Christmas Tree Fairy
Florence the Friendship Fairy
Lindsay the Luck Fairy

SCHOLASTIC

scholastic.com
rainbowmagiconline.com

There's Magic in Every Series!

The Rainbow Fairies
The Weather Fairies
The Jewel Fairies
The Pet Fairies
The Fun Day Fairies
The Petal Fairies
The Dance Fairies
The Music Fairies
The Sports Fairies
The Party Fairies
The Ocean Fairies
The Night Fairies
The Magical Animal Fairies
The Princess Fairies
The Superstar Fairies

Read them all!

SCHOLASTIC

scholastic.com
rainbowmagiconline.com

HiT entertainment

RMFAIRY7